Olvina Swims

Written and illustrated by Grace Lin

Henry Holt and Company · New York

Henry Holt and Company, LLC
Publishers since 1866
175 Fifth Avenue
New York, New York 10010
www.henryholtchildrensbooks.com

Library of Congress Cataloging-in-Publication Data
Lin, Grace. Olvina swims / Grace Lin.—1st ed.
p.   cm.
Summary: Olvina, a chicken in more ways than one, overcomes her fear of swimming
with help from her friend Hailey, a penguin, while on vacation in Hawaii.
ISBN-13: 978-0-8050-7661-5 / ISBN-10: 0-8050-7661-1
[1. Fear—Fiction. 2. Swimming—Fiction. 3. Chickens—Fiction.
4. Penguins—Fiction. 5. Hawaii—Fiction.] I. Title.
PZ7.L644Ols 2006   [Fic]—dc22   2006003430
First Edition—2007 / Designed by Donna Mark and Amelia May Anderson
The artist used gouache on Arches hot-pressed paper
to create the illustrations for this book.
Printed in the United States of America on acid-free paper. ∞

1 3 5 7 9 10 8 6 4 2

To the Blue Rose Girls, who help
this chicken do many things

Olvina and Hailey were on vacation in Hawaii
after attending the annual Bird Convention.
  Every day, they went to the beach, and Hailey
would say, "It's hot! Let's go for a swim!"
  And every day, Olvina would say, "You go ahead.
I'll stay here."

On the third day of their vacation, Hailey asked Olvina why she never wanted to go for a swim.

"Well," Olvina said, looking at the ground, "I *am* a chicken."

"Yes," Hailey prodded.

"Chickens don't swim," Olvina said and shrugged.

"Just because chickens don't swim doesn't mean they can't. It's easy—I'll teach you!"

"Teach me to swim? But I'm too scared to swim."

"Oh, Olvina!" Hailey groaned. "Don't be such a chicken."

"Where have I heard that before?" Olvina mumbled to herself.

"The first thing you need to do," Hailey said, "is get in the water."

"Me? In the water?" Olvina squeaked.

"Yes," Hailey said, shaking her head. "Olvina, don't you take baths?"

"I sponge bathe," Olvina said with dignity.

Hmm, Hailey thought. *We're going to have to start at the very beginning.*

Back at the hotel, Hailey filled the bathtub.

"There," she said to Olvina. "Get in! It's nice and warm."

Olvina took a deep breath and tested the water.

"I don't know," Olvina said as she tried to balance on the stool. But before she could . . .

OOPS!
SPLASH!

. . . she slipped and fell in!

Hailey quickly helped Olvina sit up.

Water is very wet, Olvina thought.

"Now," Hailey said, "let's try dipping your face in the water. Take a deep breath, put your head under, and blow out through your nose. When you run out of air, come back up."

Olvina was nervous but she took a deep breath, scrunched up her eyes, and—PLUNK!—put her face in the water. Carefully, Olvina opened one eye and then the other. She blew some air out of her nose and watched the bubbles stream around her. Then she lifted her head out of the water and took a big breath. She had done it!

"Good job!" Hailey said. "We'll keep working on this for a while before we try the pool."

The next day, Olvina and Hailey went to the pool.
The pool was big, and there were so many swimmers!
Olvina's legs wobbled as she stared at the blue water.

"What's that funny smell?" Olvina whispered to Hailey.

"That's just the chlorine. It keeps the pool water clean," Hailey said. "Sometimes it can sting your eyes, so wear your goggles."

Olvina put on her goggles and tightened her floaties. Hailey led her to the shallow end of the pool. Olvina clutched the stair rails and, step by step, went into the water.

"Now, dip your head under, just like in the bathtub," Hailey said.

Olvina tried to be brave. She put her head in and saw the tiled floor of the pool, her feet, and Hailey's flippers. Everything was tinted blue.

"Go ahead and let your feet float up," she heard Hailey say from above.

Olvina stretched her legs and felt herself lifted by the water. What an unusual feeling!

"Try to move your arms and legs," Hailey called.

Olvina lifted her head and kicked and wiggled. She was moving in the water!

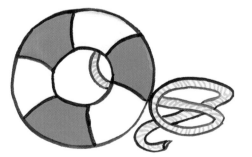

"I'm swimming!"
"That's the dog paddle," Hailey told her,
and then she giggled. "I bet that's the first
time a chicken has done the dog paddle."

For the next few days, Olvina and Hailey went to the pool and practiced. Soon, Olvina could do the backstroke *and* the dog paddle.

The day before they were to leave for home, Hailey said it was time to try swimming in the ocean.

Olvina was proud that she could swim in the pool, but the ocean?

"Come in!" Hailey called.

Oh dear, Olvina thought to herself. *I'm not sure if I can swim in moving water.*

Still, she put one foot in and then the other and felt her feet sink into the sand. The water tickled her ankles. She waded in a little deeper.

"I think I can do this," Olvina said aloud.

Olvina could taste the salty water as she dipped her head into the waves. She saw little fish and shiny colored pebbles. The water seemed to hug her. It was a wonderful feeling.

"Isn't swimming fun?" Hailey said to Olvina. "I told you chickens could swim if they really wanted to!"

"I guess chickens can do anything," Olvina said with a smile, "if they have good friends to help."